DATE DUE

GAYLORD 234

Summer's End

Maribeth Boelts

Illustrated by **Ellen Kandoian**

Houghton Mifflin Company
Boston 1995

For Adam and Hannah —M.B.

For R.J.S. —E.K.

Text copyright © 1995 by Maribeth Boelts
Illustrations copyright © 1995 by Ellen Kandoian

All rights reserved. For information about permission
to reproduce selections from this book, write to
Permissions, Houghton Mifflin Company, 215 Park Avenue
South, New York, New York 10003.

Library of Congress Cataloging-in-Publication Data

Boelts, Maribeth, 1964–
    Summer's end / Maribeth Boelts ; illustrated by Ellen Kandoian.
        p.   cm.
    Summary: With the summer almost gone, a girl thinks sadly that her
fun is over, but then she recalls some interesting things about
school.
    ISBN 0-395-70559-2
    [1. Summer—Fiction.   2. Schools—Fiction.]   I. Kandoian, Ellen,
ill.   II. Title.
PZ7.B635744Su   1995   94-14837
[E]—dc20   CIP
                               AC

Printed in the United States of America

HOR   10   9   8   7   6   5   4   3   2   1

Summer's End

The locusts are back, buzzing, and Great-Grandpa says that it
means six weeks until the frost comes, and that means summer
is almost over, and that means school is almost here.

No more baseball, swimming lessons, sparklers, camping, sweet corn, fireflies, cousins visiting . . .

. . . and no more fun. I feel like a balloon with a slow leak.

There are new shoes—the black ones with the gold streaks of lightning—and thick white socks. But my feet are summer-tough. I can run down the gravel alley behind my house, all the way to the end, without saying ouch once. The shoes and socks feel strange, and hot.

There are new shirts in the closet, and jeans, and everything
matches. Summer clothes are easier—T-shirt and shorts every day.
They're broken-in, with nothing scratchy around the neck, and no
one saying, "Be careful! Those are your new clothes!"

We go for a haircut. "How old are you?" "Did you have a good summer?" "Are you ready for school?" I answer, "Seven, yes, no," and she keeps cutting until my neck is bare and little piles of thick brown hair make the floor look furry. I put my baseball cap back on when she's through, but it's looser now.

The school gave my dad a list of all the supplies that my little sister and I will need. My sister is excited and pushes the cart around like we're getting ready for a vacation. She's careful, too. "The unicorn folder goes with the unicorn backpack. I like the rainbow pens better than the plain ones, don't you? Can I get a lunch box?" While Dad is helping her choose, I grab any old glue, the littlest box of crayons (only eight colors), and ordinary yellow pencils.

Mom says I have to clean my room before school starts. There are shells from the beach and I feel each one, and a snakeskin that the boa constrictor at the petting zoo shed, and a second place ribbon from a bike race I was in. There's a plastic treasure box with two teeth in it that the dentist had to pull, and a bucket of rocks I think are fossils.

My shelves and my desk are tidy now, but I didn't throw anything away except wrappers. Everything else was too important.

I ask Mom to give me math facts while she feeds the baby, and she makes a game out of counting all the mosquito bites on my legs. The numbers dance in my head, and I try to catch them and pull the right one down. I practice writing with one of my new pencils, but my letters look different—scraggly and tall. "Don't worry, Jill," Mom says. "It's that way for everyone after the summer." We practice until my legs feel restless from too much sitting.

The day before school, I get up early. Adam, Dana, and Reed
come over and we fill the wading pool, set up the tent for a fort,
and lay out the bases for a baseball game.

We swim until the pool is full of grass, and have a war, and play three innings, and eat a root beer popsicle, and by then it is only noon.

We sit on the porch and slap at flies and watch how carefully the man across the street mows his lawn. There is nothing left to do.

Dana and Reed go home to watch cartoons, and Adam asks me who my teacher will be.

"You get to do experiments," Adam says, riding his bike in slow, lazy circles. "And she likes rocks . . . and she lets you chew gum on your birthday."

That night I can't fall asleep. The neighborhood is quiet—everyone to bed early—but my head is noisy. I think about fireworks,
and the painted turtle I caught, and the time I hit the tennis ball
over Adam's fence. But there are other things, too . . . like the
dinosaur museum that our class visited last year, and the seeds we
planted that turned into sunflowers, and the time that Jeremy's
uncle brought in a real Native American headdress, and I got to
draw the picture for the front of his thank-you card and everyone
thought it was great.

In the morning I put on my jeans and a new soccer shirt, and I tie my lightning-streak shoes. Dad takes a picture of my sister and me like he always does, but I am the one smiling because my sister is scared about first grade.

We walk to school in a big group: Adam, Reed, and Dana in the front, my sister and me behind.

"She takes you to the dinosaur museum, and you get to plant seeds," I tell my sister, kicking a pile of yellow-tipped leaves.

We can hear the kids at school now, shouting, laughing, bouncing balls, and jumping rope. My sister sees her friend on the swing and runs ahead of me to meet her.

My feet feel like running, too, just as fast and as sure as my lightning shoes can carry me.